Written by KMH Stone
Illustrated by Emily Emerson
Published and printed through Amazon KDP
ISBN: 978-1-7398811-0-8
For information, contact: kmhstone2021@gmail.com
1st Edition

# Princess Anjula's
# Jungle Adventure

Princess Anjula lived in a beautiful palace in the Indian jungle

One day she got very bored with her toys
and decided to sneak out of the palace
and explore the jungle.

Anjula walked a short while into the jungle and saw a tiger drinking water from a pond.

The tiger bowed in front of the princess once he saw her.

"Where can I take you, my princess?" the tiger asked.
"I want to go deep into the jungle," Anjula said.

"Your wish is my command, climb my back and
I will take you there in a jiffy," the tiger said.

Anjula climbed the tiger's back and off they sped through the jungle until they reached a river.

"I can't cross the river my princess, but I will get my friend the crocodile to take you across," the tiger said.

The tiger called for the crocodile, who quickly swam towards them. "On my back your highness," the crocodile said. The crocodile was grinning with all his teeth.

Anjula jumped on his back and they got to the other side of the river in no time.

On the other side of the river
Anjula was met by a blue and yellow python.

"Princess, I will take you to a ruby tree full of rubies," the snake said. "Yes please! My parents don't have enough rubies as it is," replied Anjula.

The snake slithered at lightning speed with Anjula on his back as he took her deeper into the jungle.

Anjula was dazzled by the rubies once they reached the tree. She became giddy with excitement and was stunned by the tree's beauty. The rubies glistened so beautifully in the sunlight.

High up in the branches were a troop of monkeys.

The monkeys came down to perform magic tricks for the princess.

The monkeys were ever so kind. After entertaining the princess, they collected a huge bag full of rubies from the treetop for her.

"Princess, since you love rubies just look at the tree to your left full of gold bangles and the tree to your right is full of sapphires," said one of the monkeys.

'Princess, there is also another tree behind them that is full of emeralds. Do you want us to collect a bag of each?" another monkey asked.

"Yes, please," replied Anjula.

As the monkeys collected the treasures from the trees, Anjula heard a loud trumpet sound from the trunk of an elephant who was marching towards them.

The elephant looked small in the distance, but Anjula realized how huge she was when she got closer.

"Princess, I hear the king and queen calling for you with my large ears. I think it is time for you to go back home. Climb on my back and I will take you back to the palace now," the elephant said.

As she rode home saddled with all the treasures she found in the jungle, Anjula saw 20 peacocks by the river bed. Their wonderful shimmering feathers were something to behold.

"Do you want to live in the palace with me?
There is plenty of food and water there," Anjula asked.

"Yes please!" the peacocks replied.

All the animals she met on her adventure
followed Anjula triumphantly into the palace.

Anjula's parents were happy to see her safe and sound, but were shocked to see all her new friends as well as the huge bags bursting with treasure.

"Where have you been?" her parents asked.

"On an adventure," replied Anjula.

# The end

Printed in Great Britain
by Amazon

77469671R00018